Llyfrgell Sir POWYS County Library
Llandrindod Wells LD1 5LD

www.powys.gov.uk/libraries

This book must be returned by the last date stamped above.
Rhaid dychwelyd y llyfr hwn erbyn y dyddiad diwethaf a stampiwyd uchod.

A charge will be made for any lost, damaged or overdue books.
Codir tâl os bydd llyfr wedi ei golli neu ei ni weidio neu heb ei ddychwelyd mewn pryd.

D0492866

HOPSCOTCH HISTORIES

The King
and the
Great Fire

by Lynne Benton
Illustrated by Peter Cottrill

W
FRANKLIN WATTS
LONDON·SYDNEY

About this book

Some of the characters in this book are made up, but the story is based on real events in history. King Charles II (1630–1685) had only been king for six years when the Great Fire of London broke out in 1666. It started in the king's baker's house in Pudding Lane and raged for four days and three nights, destroying many homes, churches and public buildings including St Paul's Cathedral. The king helped fight the fire himself and made sure all the people had food and shelter. He then had to face the task of rebuilding London.

First published in 2009 by
Franklin Watts
338 Euston Road
London
NW1 3BH

Franklin Watts Australia
Level 17/207 Kent Street
Sydney
NSW 2000

Text © Lynne Benton 2009
Illustrations © Peter Cottrill 2009

The right of Lynne Benton to be identified as the author
and Peter Cottrill as illustrator of this Work has been asserted
in accordance with the Copyright, Designs and Patents Act, 1988.

A CIP catalogue record for this book is available
from the British Library.

ISBN 978 0 7496 8575 1 (hbk)
ISBN 978 0 7496 8581 2 (pbk)

Series Editor: Melanie Palmer
Series Advisor: Dr Barrie Wade
Series Designer: Peter Scoulding

Printed in China

Franklin Watts is a division of
Hachette Children's Books,
an Hachette UK company
www.hachette.co.uk

King Charles II was asleep after
a busy day ruling England.

Just then a servant rushed in.

"Your Majesty!" he cried,

"London is on fire!"

"Oh no!" gasped the King.

"I must help put the fire out."

King Charles hurried out of the palace towards the fire. Suddenly a boy ran round the corner, straight into his path.

The horse shied.

"Look where you're going,
boy!" cried the King.

Then a blazing timber fell
from a roof. It landed right in
front of the horse.

"Zounds!" said Charles.

"You have saved your king's life!"

The boy gasped. "Are you really the King of England?" he asked.
"Yes," said Charles, "who are you?"
"I'm Will," said the boy, shyly.

"I'm going to help put out the fire," said the King. "Can you help me, Will?"

"Yes," Will said, happily.

They rode past burning buildings.
People were rushing out, carrying
their possessions.

"Where will they go?" asked Will.
"I've ordered tents for them, away
from the fire," said the King.

"They'll be hungry, too," said Will.

"Good thinking!" said the King.

"I'll order bread for them as well.

Now we must hurry to the river."

At the river, lots of people were filling buckets and throwing water onto the flames.

The King and Will rushed to help.
Everyone was pleased to see the
King. "Now London will be saved,"
they cheered.

The King watched the fire raging. "We should blow up some houses to stop the fire spreading," a man told him.

The King agreed. He wrote an order down and gave it to Will. "Take this message to the Lord Mayor," he said, "and hurry!"

Will ran through the streets.
Even the ground was hot,
so he had to run very fast.

The air was thick with smoke,
and the sky was red with fire.

At last Will found the Lord Mayor.
"Message from the King!" he said,
out of breath.

The Lord Mayor read the note. "It will cost too much to rebuild all those houses," he grumbled.

Will rushed back to the King with the Lord Mayor's reply. So Charles gave his own orders.

Soon sailors came back from the
dockyards with lots of gunpowder.

They heard a huge explosion.

"Well done, Will," said the King.

"That will stop the fire spreading any further. Now we must put out the rest."

They worked for three more days, until the fire was finally put out. "You're a good worker, Will," said the King. "Would you like to work in my kitchen at the palace?"

"Yes please," said Will, grinning.
"I'll try not to burn anything!"

Puzzle 1

Put these pictures in the correct order.

Which event do you think is most important?

Now try writing the story in your own words!

Puzzle 2

Word Bank

Bucket
Dockyard
Gunpowder
Letter
Mayor
River

What do these pictures tell you about King

Charles II and the way of life at the time?

How are things different today?

You can use the word bank to help you.

Answers

Puzzle 1

The correct order is: 1d, 2e, 3f, 4a, 5c, 6b.

Puzzle 2

Life was very different during King Charles II's lifetime.
Think about buildings, fire brigades, palaces and clothes.
To find out more, try this book:

The Great Fire of London, (Ways Into History),

Sally Hewitt, Franklin Watts, 2009

Look out for more Hopscotch Histories:

Henry VIII Has to Choose
ISBN 978 0 7496 8573 7*
ISBN 978 0 7496 8579 9

The King and the Great Fire
ISBN 978 0 7496 8575 1*
ISBN 978 0 7496 8581 2

Florence and the Drummer Boy
ISBN 978 0 7496 8574 4*
ISBN 978 0 7496 8580 5

Ben's Escape from the Blitz
ISBN 978 0 7496 8578 2*
ISBN 978 0 7496 8584 3

The Song of Boudica
ISBN 978 0 7496 8576 8*
ISBN 978 0 7496 8582 9

Eric Bloodaxe, the Viking King
ISBN 978 0 7496 8577 5*
ISBN 978 0 7496 8583 6

Toby and the Great Fire of London
ISBN 978 0 7496 7410 6

Hoorah for Mary Seacole
ISBN 978 0 7496 7413 7

Remember Remember the 5th of November
ISBN 978 0 7496 7414 4

Pocahontas the Peacemaker
ISBN 978 0 7496 7080 1*
ISBN 978 0 7496 7411 3

Grandma's Seaside Bloomers
ISBN 978 0 7496 7412 0

Tutankhamun and the Golden Chariot
ISBN 978 0 7496 7084 9*
ISBN 978 0 7496 7415 1

For more Hopscotch books go to: www.franklinwatts.co.uk

*hardback